JAMAL'S BUSY DAY

by Wade Hudson
illustrated by George Ford

Printed in the USA. First Edition 10 9 8 7 6 5 4 3
Library of Congress Catalog Number 90-81646
ISBN: 0-940975-21-1 (library edition)   0-940975-24-6 (paper)

JUST US BOOKS
Orange, New Jersey
1991

Mommy, Daddy and I start our work day early. We wash up, shave, and brush our teeth.

Then we put on our work clothes.
I always finish first.

Before we leave for work, we eat a healthy breakfast.

We have to be ready for our busy day.

My daddy is an architect.
He makes drawings to guide
the people who build houses.

He works hard.

My mommy is an accountant.
She's always busy with numbers.
Mommy works very hard.

I work hard, too.

I work with numbers.

I make drawings.

I try experiments.

I do research.

Then there are meetings to attend.

My supervisor always calls on me
for a helping hand.

And sometimes I have to settle disagreements between my co-workers. There is always work to do.

Getting home is not easy, either.
The bus is always crowded.

But when I get there, I relax.
I have to unwind.

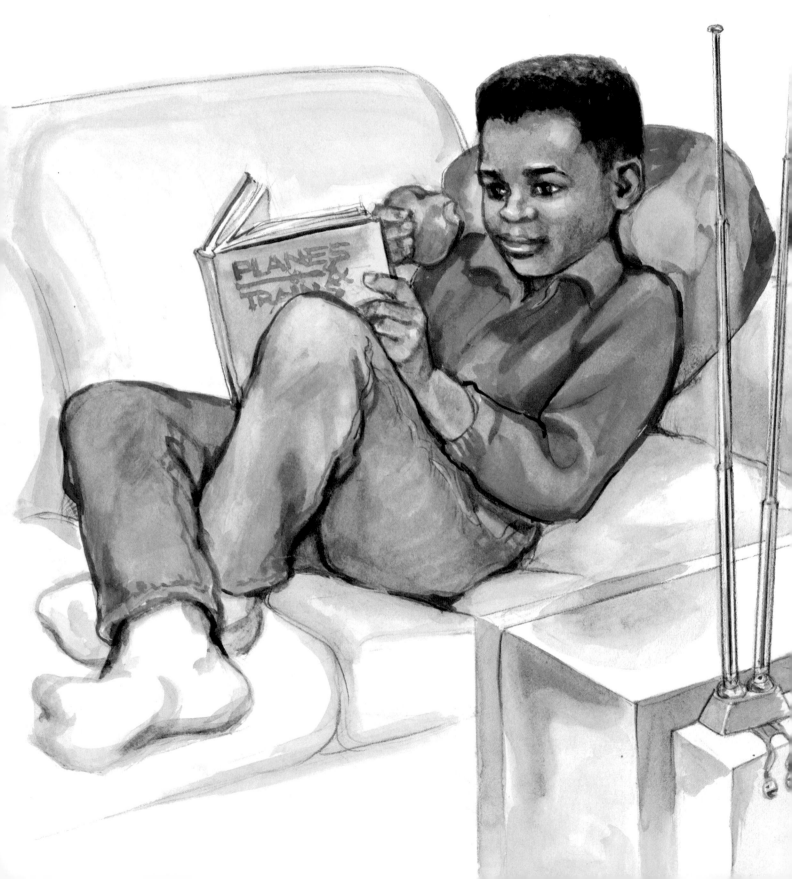

Sometimes I bring work home.
Reports are always due.

Then I shoot a few hoops.

Soon, it's time for dinner.
We all help.
I set the table.

Later, Daddy and Mommy talk
about their busy day.

I say, "I know just what you mean.
I've had a busy day myself."

But I can't wait until tomorrow.

WADE HUDSON is a writer whose published works for children include the popular *Afro-Bets® Book of Black Heroes from A to Z, Beebe's Lonely Saturday* and the play, *Freedom Star*. He attended Southern University in Louisiana and the Television and Film School at WNET-Channel 13 in New York City. *Sam Carter Belongs Here, The Return* and *A House Divided* are among the plays written by Mr. Hudson that have been produced on stage. A former public relations specialist, he and his wife, Cheryl, founded Just Us Books.

GEORGE FORD is a distinguished artist who has illustrated more than two dozen books for young readers. He grew up in the Brownsville and Bedford-Stuyvesant sections of Brooklyn and spent some of his early years on the West Indian island of Barbados. Among the books Mr. Ford has illustrated are *Bright Eyes, Brown Skin, Afro-Bets® First Book About Africa, Muhammad Ali, Far Eastern Beginnings, Paul Robeson, Ego Tripping* and *Ray Charles,* for which he won the American Library Association's Coretta Scott King Award.